André Dahan
The Cat and the Dog

What a warm and sunny day!

Perhaps this dog would like to play.

Oops! You didn't find that fun?

I guess that I had better run.

On this ball, I'll bounce away
And you won't catch me, not today!

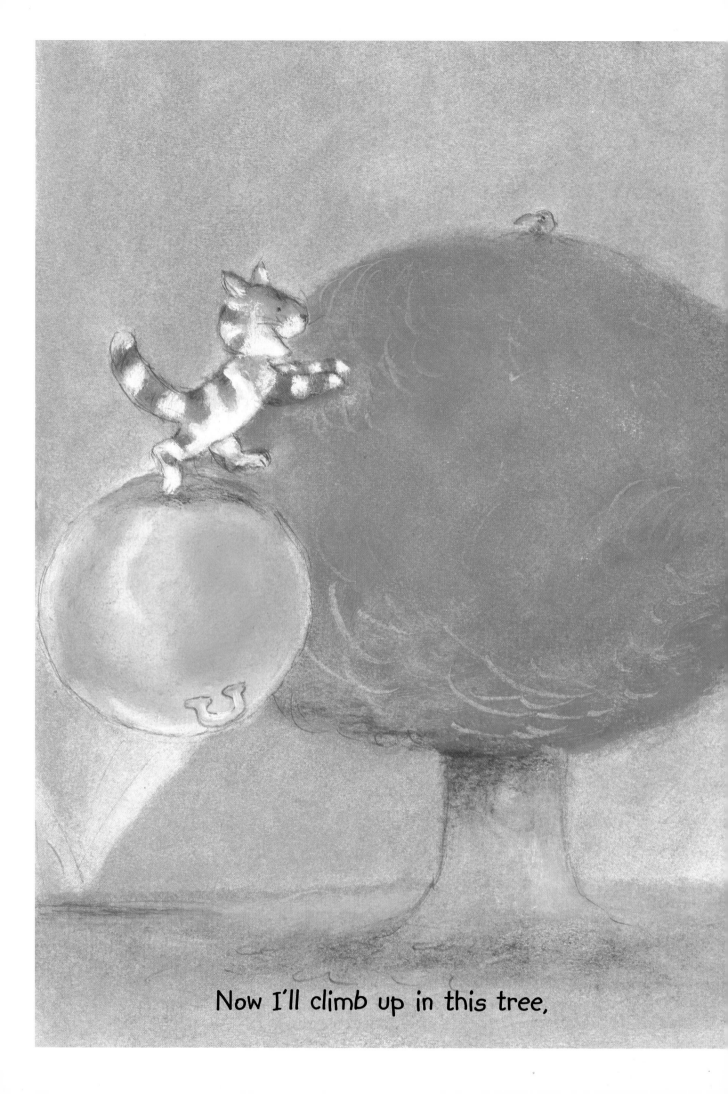

Now I'll climb up in this tree,

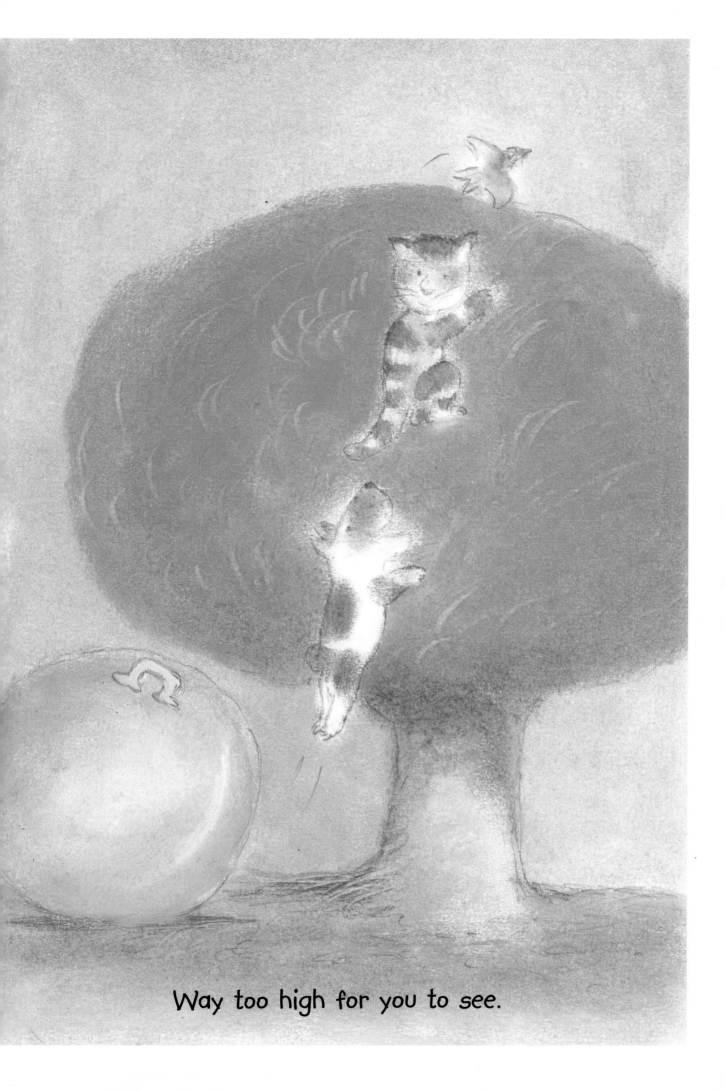

Way too high for you to see.

I'll hide as quiet as a mouse,

Then jump on top of this small house.

Oh look! I see a little boat.

I hope that you know how to float.

You must be so very wet,

But you'll not catch me. No, not yet.

I will climb up on this slide,

Then take it down for a quick ride.

And as you make your way on down,

I will swing right off the ground.

Oh, dear me!

Is this the end?

Why no, of course. I've found a friend!